DANIEL E BROWN

ELI—PRIDE OF THE YAZOO RIVER

Eli—Pride of the Yazoo River

v4.0

Outskirts Press, Inc.
http://www.outskirtspress.com

Paperback ISBN: 978-1-9772-0453-0
Hardback ISBN: 978-1-9772-0454-7

Library of Congress Control Number: 2018911654

Illustrations by: Victor Guiza.

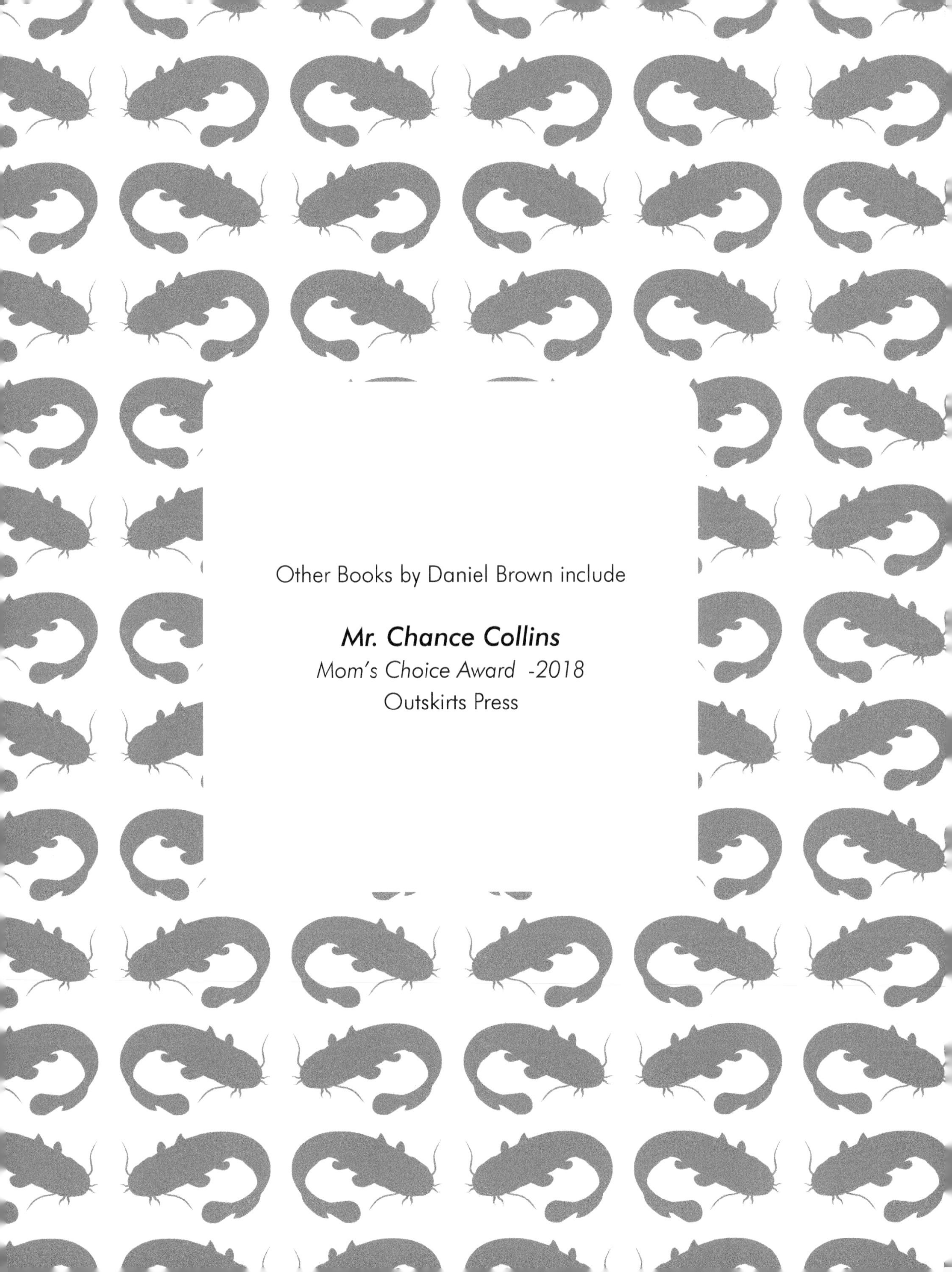

Other Books by Daniel Brown include

Mr. Chance Collins
Mom's Choice Award -2018
Outskirts Press

Thirty-four miles northwest of Jackson, Mississippi is the small village of Satartia. It's pronounced Suh-tar-shuh. Someone once told me that the name means Pumpkins in the ancient Yazoo Indian language. If you call the town Sat-ar-tee-uh, folks will either correct you or just give you a look as if to say, "What dump truck full of turnips did you just fall out of?"

Satartia is a one of a kind Southern town. This little town is located at the very edge of the Mississippi Delta. Huge 200-year-old oak trees stand guard on either side of Plum Street, which, by the way, is one of only a few streets. Satartia also has a lift bridge crossing the Yazoo River. It was built in 1976. At the time, it was sort of an engineering wonder. But the best part of this sleepy little town is what lives under this ole bridge. Nope, it's not a troll... (that's a different story!) but it is quite a curiosity. You can even call it a mystery. The mystery's name? Folks just call him Eli.

For over twenty years, kids and grown-up kids (called adults) have gone down to the muddy banks of the Yazoo River to fish for Eli. As far as anyone can tell, Eli appears to be a GY-NOR-MOUS catfish. Most of the men down at the General Store guess ole Eli to weigh near 'bout one hundred fifty pounds! Depends on who's telling the story when you ask about him. You see, just about everyone around Satartia has tried to catch ole Eli, but no one has been able to get that rascal out of that river. Eli is too big, too powerful, and he's got a mind of his own. By the way, his mind tells him that he is happy right where he is ... *in the water, under that bridge!*

Eli is big enough to break just about every kind of fishing line. His jaws can cut a fishing line like a hot knife going through soft butter at the Thanksgiving dinner table. Most of the time, the Yazoo River isn't very deep under the bridge. Now, that can change after a heavy rain. The last time that I laid my eyes on the river, it was about 100 feet from one side to the other. Because ole Eli is so big, whenever he moves about in calm water, it looks like a submarine is prowling about in the river. Eli actually makes a small wave on the surface of the muddy water.

Over the years, a lot of men have tried to catch ole Eli. They have even tried to use heavy steel fishing cables. Eli is too smart for that trick. He is not dumb. But, speaking of dumb, one time a crazy fella from Possum Bend, Mississippi told everyone he could wrestle Eli right out of that river. He had this plan of tying a rope around his waist and having someone hold the other end of the rope to keep him from going under the water for too long. This crazy fella's name was Cletus Ray Johnson. Cletus would sometimes act like he didn't have a brain. Some folks would say, "If he did, it must not be any bigger than a butter bean!"

If you believed that Cletus Ray had any chance to catch ole Eli, then you would probably believe that fried cotton is good to eat! Cletus Ray was long on courage but short on "smarts." Folks around Possum Bend used to say, "Cletus Ray was so goofy that he could not find his back pocket with two hands, a shovel, and a flashlight." Not exactly sure what that truly means, but it does qualify for "goofy" in my mind.

I remember many years ago, back in 1987, June 7th, to be exact, the whole town of Satartia, all sixty-eight of them, gathered at the river banks to watch Cletus Ray Johnson go up against the mighty Eli. Eli was, without question, the overwhelming favorite of the folks gathered that day. It seemed as if folks around Satartia didn't like the idea of someone from Possum Bend coming over to their town to try and catch their living legend.

Come Again
PEACHES
APPLES
EGGS
25-CENTS
SALTINE
CRACKERS
SALT
PEPPER
SUGAR
Drink
YAZOO
COLA
POTATOES

My brother certainly did not care much for Cletus Ray. He told me that Cletus walked in the General Store and smelled worse than skunk perfume! Everyone stood up from their seats and left the store in a hurry. He said you should have seen the frowns on their faces. They hurried out the door, leaving Mr. Ragland behind. I suppose someone had to watch the store. Mr. Ragland held his nose, frowning, and offered to buy Cletus a bar of 99 and 44/100ths percent pure soap. Cletus just shrugged his shoulders and said, "Never use the stuff." Whew...!

It took two minutes to get Cletus Ray to leave that store. To Mr. Ragland, it seemed like thirty minutes. After Cletus Ray left the General Store, Mr. Ragland ran home and took his own bath!

It all came down to one decision. If anyone was to catch ole Eli, the townspeople wanted it to be someone from Satartia. This was THEIR fish!

Cletus Ray walked from the General Store down to the river with all the eyes of Satartia watching him. Very carefully, a Boy Scout from Troop 9 (Madison Miss.) tied a knot known as two half-hitches around Cletus Ray's waist. Cletus was pleased with the Boy Scout's efforts. He waded right into the Yazoo River. A man held onto the other end of the rope, *juuuuust* in case Cletus Ray needed any help. Cletus leaned down and reached with his hands, feeling around in the side of the river bank. He reached a big pipe where ole Eli had been known to take a nap or two. Cletus began to smile.

Now, Cletus had what they call in Yazoo County "summer teeth." Some are there AND…some are not. Cletus lost his two front teeth when he was seventeen years old while he was out teasing some cows in a farmer's pasture. It seems no one told Cletus about the bull that was out in that same pasture. Cletus was fast but, on that day, the bull was *juuust a little faster*. That bull sent Cletus Ray ten feet up in to a tree. Yep, he will tell you that is how he lost his two "toofers."

Now, back to our story....

I don't know how you wake up from a nap when you got someone a-reachin' and a-grabbin' onto you, but ole Eli proved that he was a little grumpy when he first woke up. As a matter of fact, he was downright upset about Cletus Ray being his alarm clock. Instantly, the water began to boil. A column of water, Eli, and a very surprised Cletus Ray shot up about five feet into the air. Like a bull rider at the Yazoo County rodeo, he rode on the back of that mighty catfish! Ole Eli gave Cletus Ray a tour of the river. He went from one side of the river to the other. Everyone was cheering for Eli, especially Mr. Ragland. He leaned over and said, "This may be the closest Cletus Ray comes to taking a bath this whole month." In short, nobody wanted Cletus Ray to win his fight with Eli. Mostly, because if he WERE caught, this local legend would be over. Eli pulled Cletus Ray's stinky body *all over the river!* The big ole fish was slashing and tearing at the water, dragging him around as if he were a child's toy. Eli even showed Cletus what *the bottom of the river* looks like. Cletus had so much mud in his ears that you could have planted cotton in there!

Finally, Eli decided that this game of piggyback was becoming a bit of a nuisance. With a burst of power and speed, Eli swam to the river's edge and with his powerful tail, Eli spanked Cletus Ray right off his back. He flew in the air about ten feet up the river bank and landed in Mrs. Hart's prize-winning rose bushes. "YEEEE OOOOOW!" cried Cletus Ray. "That fish plays mighty rough!"

Everyone in town had a great big rib-rattling, tummy-tumbling laugh at crazy Cletus Ray Johnson. Cletus wasn't laughing, though. Shoot-fire, he had so many thorns in his britches that he would not be able to sit down for a whole week!

Cletus lowered his head and snorted the rest of the Yazoo River mud out of his nose as he made his way back home to Possum Bend. The good folks in Satartia went back to their chores, and everything pretty much returned to normal.

Back at the General Store, the old men went back to playing checkers, drinking sweet tea, fussing about State and Ole Miss football games, and reflecting on how Eli had showed everyone WHO WAS BOSS!

"Hey, Granddad!"

A voice popped up as the General Store's screen door opened and slammed shut with a loud rattle. One of the old fellas leaned back from his checker board table and said, "Well, hey there, sweetheart."

The young lady was the brown-haired, brown-eyed, pony-tailed granddaughter of the gentleman. Her name was Victoria, but her Grandfather called her "Tori." In fact, everyone in town called her Tori.

"Granddad, are ya winning?" Tori asked.

"No, lil' darlin'. Mr. Davis may be a-cheatin', but I can't seem to catch him."

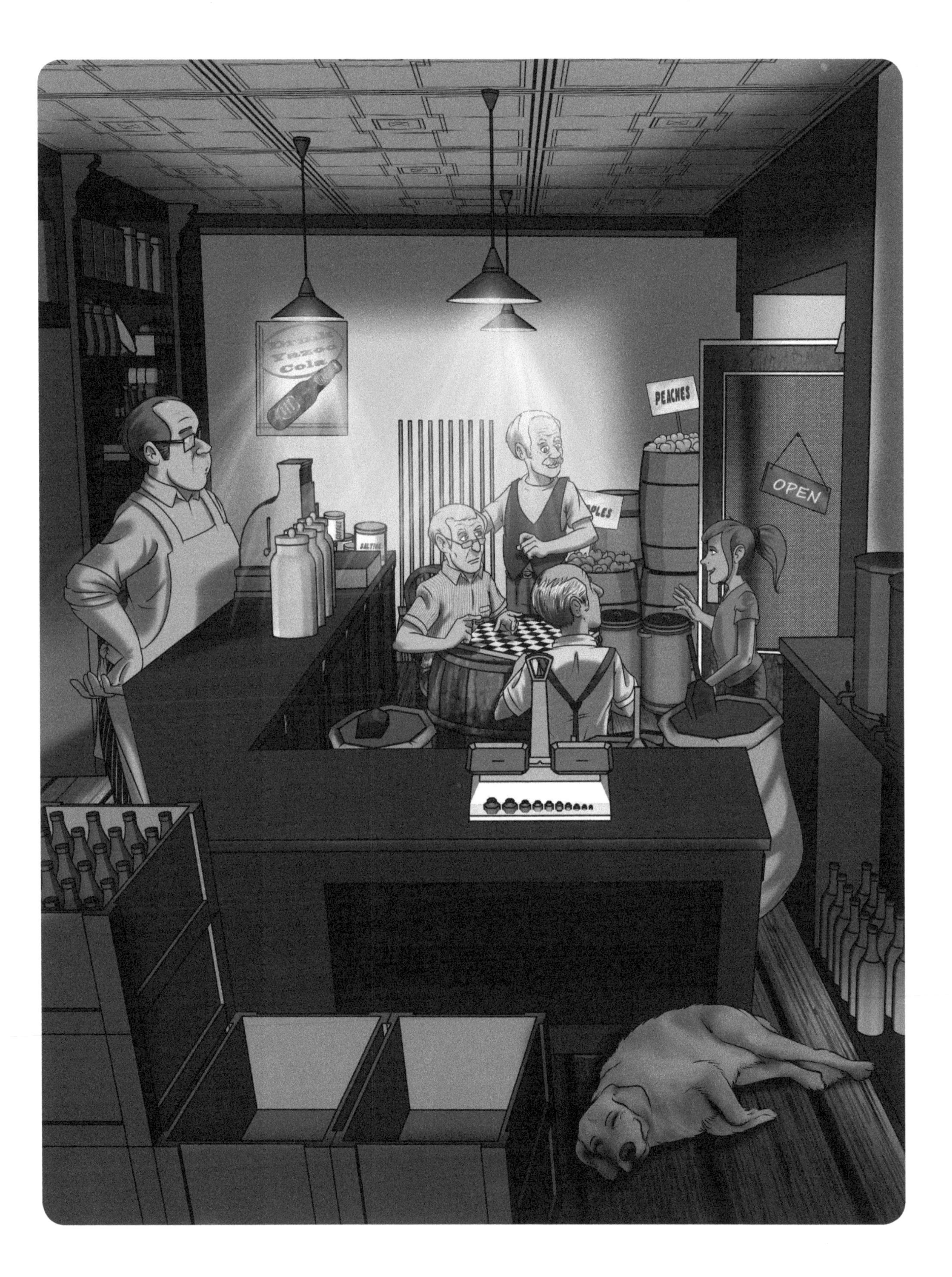
Yazoo
Cola
PEACHES
OPEN

Mr. Davis winked at Tori and said, "Mornin', Tori." He greeted everyone by saying "Mornin'," even if it were 3 o'clock in the afternoon, he would still say "Mornin'." That was his custom, and nobody seemed to care or even notice.

"Granddad, have you seen Timmy?"

"Not recently, but I heard someone say that he was chopping cotton over across the bridge."

Tori started for the door as her Grandfather returned his attention back to the checker board. "Thanks—bye, y'all."

Everyone around the table stopped what they were doing, looked up, and returned her goodbye.

Tori grabbed her bicycle and pedaled out onto Plum Street. She rode over to the bridge and towards the cotton field on the other side. It took all of three minutes to find Timmy. He looked tired as he looked up from chopping cotton. He leaned on his hoe where he had been working. "Timmy, whatcha doing?"

He smiled a tired smile and said, "I am trying to earn enough money to buy some lumber so I can build a big ole raft for the river."

"A raft?" Tori asked.

"Yep, I am going after Eli," Timmy proudly announced.

"You? Are you out of your mind? You saw what that fish did to Cletus Ray Johnson!" she exclaimed. "He will pull you off of that raft in no time at all."

"Eli will not," Timmy fired back at her. "Matter of fact, when I get paid, I will have $28.75. That will be plenty enough to build what I need. I will use logs, nails, and some long boards. By the end of this week, I will have the best raft on the Yazoo River."

Friday arrived, and Timmy rode into Jackson with his Dad. They rode in the family's 1967 Chevy pickup truck. His Dad called the truck "Ole Blue." Folks around Satartia never could understand that name, because the pickup was painted Red.

JACKSON
EAT
LUMBER

Yazoo Dream

Timmy only spent $18.53 at the lumber yard. They loaded up Ole Blue with boards, rope, and long nails. On the way home, Timmy's Dad asked him how he planned to catch that big fish. He was concerned for his son's safety (and rightly so). His Dad listened to Timmy's whole plan and added a few suggestions of his own.

Father and son worked together most of that Saturday. By late afternoon, they had finished. Together, they drove the raft the short distance down to the river's edge. The raft was ten feet wide and twelve feet long. Timmy placed a flag on the back of the raft that read YAZOO DREAM. It was a fitting name. The raft was well built. Timmy was proud of his project, as several curious folks stopped what they were doing and helped them slide the raft into the Yazoo River.

At first, Tori didn't think that the raft was going to float. She hid herself behind a big oak tree and watched from a distance. But the Yazoo Dream was indeed a marvelous raft. She found herself a bit wishful that she could be on the Yazoo Dream too. Timmy looked proud as he pushed himself along the river with a long pole Mr. Cresswell had given him. Tori wished that she could go with Timmy to catch the mighty fish. Timmy pushed the Yazoo Dream over to the river bank and Tori walked down to greet him.

"Timmy, how are you going to catch Eli?"

"It's pretty simple, really. I am going to train Eli to come to the raft."

Tori just laughed out loud at him. "Oh sure, you're going to lean over the water and say Here Fishy-Wishy. Come here, boy. Sit. Roll over. Shake. Now, go get me the newspaper. Good Eli, good fella."

"I am NOT kidding!" Timmy insisted in a strong voice. "I saw a movie at school that said that fish can be trained to come to a noise if a reward, like food, is thrown into the water. So, every day for the next month, I am going to toss gross, slimy chicken livers into the water while I am making a loud noise on the raft. My Dad says that chicken livers are like candy to a catfish. They love 'em."

"So how are you going to make a noise on the raft?" Tori asked. "I am going to hit the side of the raft with a pipe. The movie at school said that fish can hear noises in the water up to a mile away. If I reward ole Eli enough, maybe .... *juuuuust* maybe, he will come to me like a puppy dog."

Now Tori was interested. "Will you need any help?" she asked hopefully.

"Sure thing. I will need someone to help me make noise or toss chicken livers into the river," Timmy said.

So every day at 5:30, Timmy's Dad returned home from work with chicken livers for Timmy to give to Eli. By 6:00, Timmy and Tori pushed the Yazoo Dream away from the river bank.

A week passed, and Eli was nowhere to be found. Then, one calm Tuesday evening, at exactly 6:14 p.m., Timmy began to bang on the side of his raft. Tori had now grown accustomed to the stinky and slimy chicken livers. She was not paying close attention when a small wave in the water began to move from the other side of the river to the raft. The movement of the water then began to take the shape of a huge, monstrous black object. The giant fish came up to the surface, and Tori just about froze with fright.

"Tori. Tori...don't be scared. Throw Eli the chicken livers. Quick."

Plop. Plop. Plop. The chicken livers hit the water and the big fish opened his mouth to gobble up the reward. His big mouth opened and closed like a garage door at home. His mouth was easily as big as a basketball. He actually ate the livers like a puppy dog waiting for the next treat. Tori tossed Eli the last liver that she had. They waited quietly for a minute or two and the big fish slowly disappeared to the bottom of the river. Timmy and Tori just sat there grinning at what they had just seen. Timmy's plan worked!

Yazoo
Dream

The next day they were both very excited as they pushed the Yazoo Dream away from the river bank. Within a minute or two, Eli was back at their side when Timmy sounded the signal on the edge of the raft. Ole Eli gobbled up every treat he was offered. (Eli even brought a few of his buddies to join him.)

Each day, during the next week, the mighty fish appeared within five minutes' time from Timmy's first signal. The day he had waited for was now here. Timmy had everything he needed to catch Eli. Timmy and Tori were both silent as the raft was pushed out into the current of the river. Neither of them felt like talking. They both were thinking, *How can we possibly stand to catch a big fish that is coming to our raft like a puppy dog goes to his food bowl?* Eli surely thought of them as his friends. Is this how you treat your friends? Of course not. This pursuit of the legend needed to end.

Suddenly, a sound caught Timmy and Tori's attention. It was the roar of a slow-moving diesel engine. A river barge was slowly coming their direction. Ugly black smoke was coming out of the single smoke stack high above the barge. It was coming right toward them. On the front of the barge was Cletus Ray Johnson. He was waving the Captain onward. They were pulling a big net behind that old barge.

"Hey! That is against the law! You can't catch Eli in a net!"

Cletus Ray just sneered at the kids. The barge kept coming closer and closer.

"Quick, let's push the raft over to that little slough." (Slough is pronounced "slew.") "It will be way too shallow for that barge!" Timmy pointed out.

Now, just in case you are not from around these parts, you may not know what a "slough" is. It is a place where the water is just not very deep. Much like a swamp. For sure ... *no barge can go through a slough*. Hah!

Yazoo Dream

Timmy and Tori pushed their raft into the slough, and Timmy began to hit the side of his raft with the pipe. They were trying their best to call Eli over to them and away from Cletus Ray Johnson. Tori yelled out, "Hit the raft faster!" Timmy was rapping out his signal as fast as he could to try to move Eli toward them and away from that net.

The barge was now even with their raft. Suddenly, a wave moved from the middle of the Yazoo River towards the kids. Cletus Ray was watching with great anticipation.

"Look, Tori!" Timmy pointed. Eli had edged up to the side of the raft in the shallow water. When the big barge was about to pass under the lift bridge, Cletus Ray motioned for the net that they were pulling behind the barge to be raised. Timmy and Tori couldn't help but laugh when they could see that there were only a few confused fish and three dizzy turtles in the net. Tori tossed a few chicken livers to their friend Eli.

"I am sorry, Timmy, but I want you stop trying to catch Eli. Last Sunday, the preacher said God places special things in your life for a reason. And, when He does that, we should pay close attention to what those 'Special Things' are."

"You're right, Tori. The truth is...I did change my mind. When I saw Cletus Ray on the front of that barge, I decided that it would NOT be right for anyone to catch the big fella."

Tori tossed Eli the remaining chicken livers, and Timmy guided the raft back over to where they kept the Yazoo Dream tied up.

The next day was Saturday. Timmy and his Dad got to talking about what they should do. They needed a plan to save Eli. Timmy's Dad borrowed a motorboat. Tori helped them as they loaded the boat with ten pounds of chicken livers. They launched the boat into the river near the bridge. It would be a very long day.

Timmy banged on the side of the boat, and sure enough, Eli appeared at their side. Carefully and slowly, Timmy and Tori guided Eli down river by giving him all the chicken livers that a big catfish would ever want! A few hours later, the boat and the river

current arrived at a place where the Yazoo River flows into the Big Sunflower River. The three of them in the boat sat quietly for a moment until Timmy took the rest of the chicken livers and tossed them into a spot where the Yazoo River current meets the Big Sunflower River current. Eli was accustomed to the sound of the splash, and he swam over to get his reward. They all watched closely as Eli's big tail pushed him into the current of his new home in the Big Sunflower River.

That big, beautiful catfish, the Legend of Satartia, their friend... disappeared out of sight. Everyone just looked at each other for a moment or two before Timmy's Dad pointed the boat back upstream to head back home. A tired Timmy said, "This is what the big fella deserves. A mighty fish ... in a mighty river. Goodbye, Eli. Goodbye, my friend."

The End

CPSIA information can be obtained
at www.ICGtesting.com
Printed in the USA
BVHW061055010323
659483BV00002B/46